STONE ARCH BOOKS
a capstone imprint

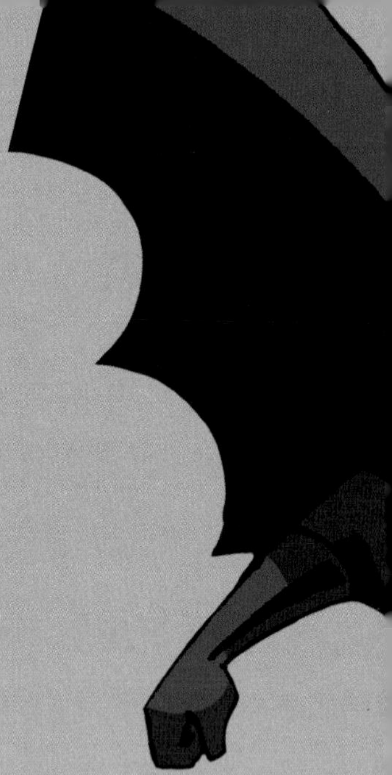

STONE ARCH BOOKS™

Published in 2015
by Stone Arch Books
A Capstone Imprint
1710 Roe Crest Drive
North Mankato, MN 56003
www.capstonepub.com

Originally published by DC Comics in
the U.S. in single magazine form as Beware
the Batman #3.

DC Comics
1700 Broadway, New York, NY 10019
A Warner Bros. Entertainment Company

Cataloging-in-Publication Data is available
at the Library of Congress website:
ISBN: 978-1-4342-9740-2 (library binding)

Summary: Tobias Whale has his sights set
on the secret store of weapons sunk under
Gotham City's bay. Whale is ready to salvage
the ship, but Batman also has plans to secure
the cache for safekeeping. When the two men
collide beneath the bay, only one man -- or one
Whale -- will prevail.

STONE ARCH BOOKS
Ashley C. Andersen Zantop *Publisher*
Michael Dahl *Editorial Director*
Sean Tulien *Editor*
Heather Kindseth *Creative Director*
Alison Thiele and Peggie Carley *Designers*
Tori Abraham *Production Specialist*

DC COMICS
Alex Antone *Original U.S. Editor*

Printed in China by Nordica.
0914/CA21401510
092014 008470NORDS15

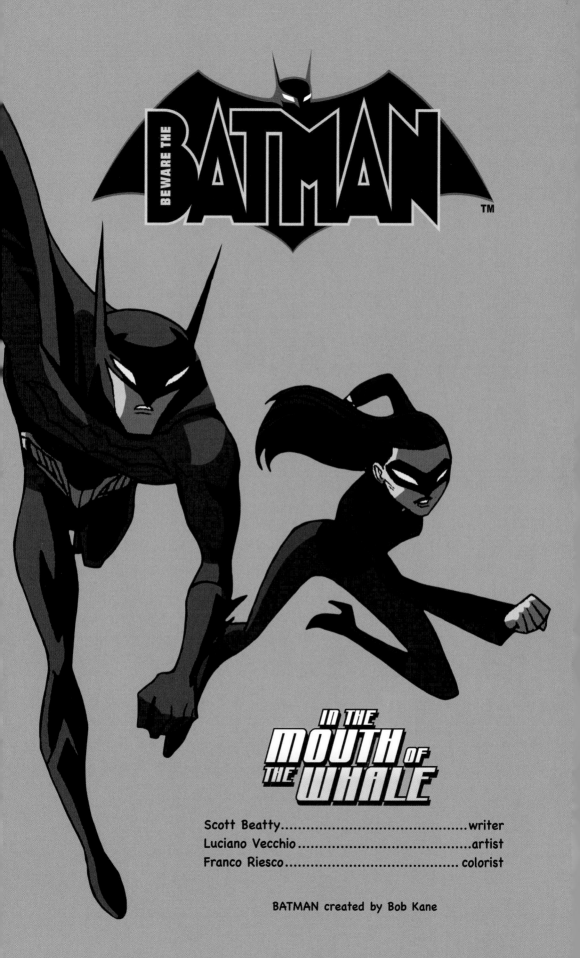

BEWARE THE BATMAN ™

IN THE MOUTH OF THE WHALE

Scott Beatty..writer
Luciano Vecchio..artist
Franco Riesco..colorist

BATMAN created by Bob Kane

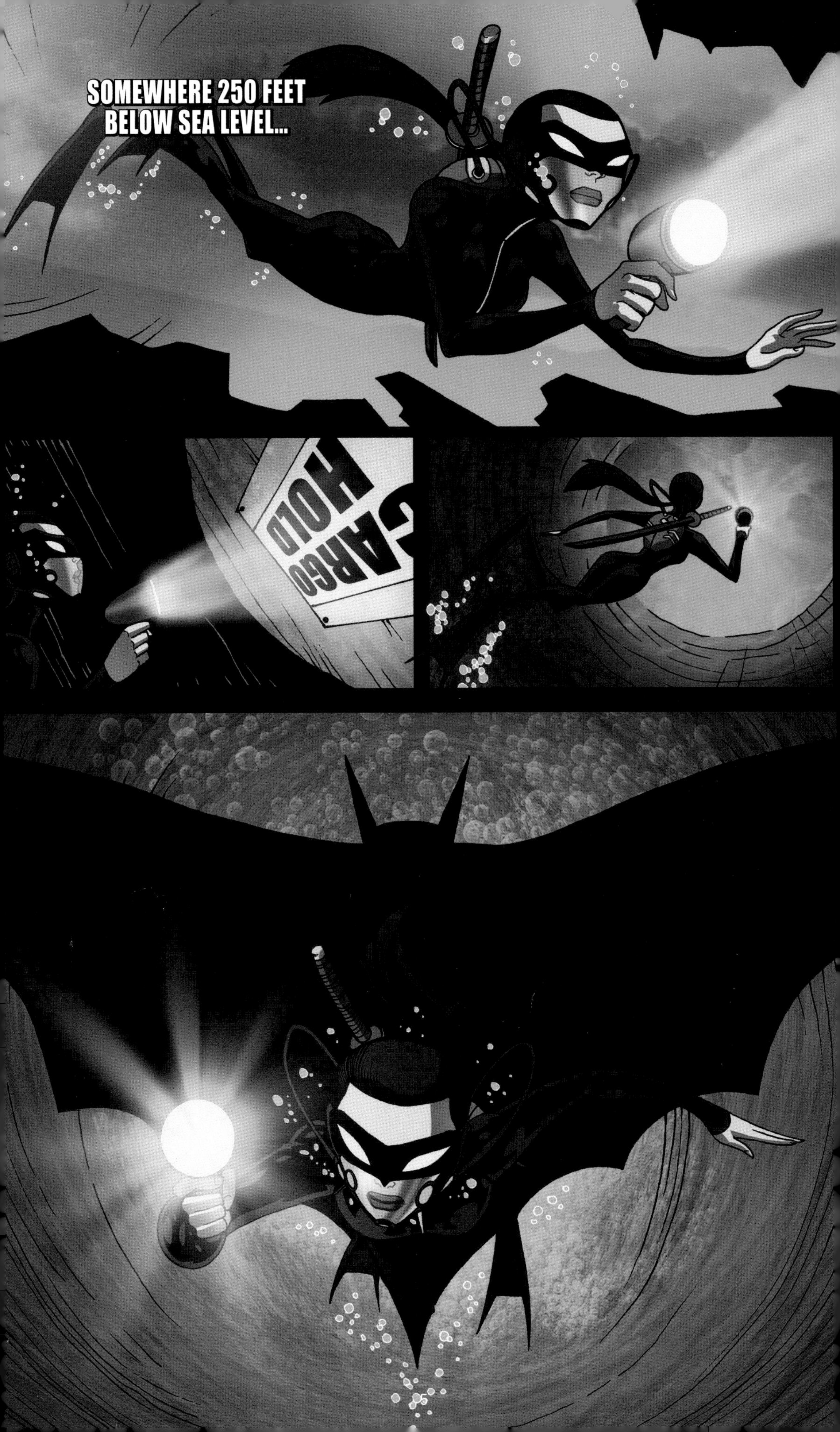
SOMEWHERE 250 FEET BELOW SEA LEVEL...
CARGO HOLD

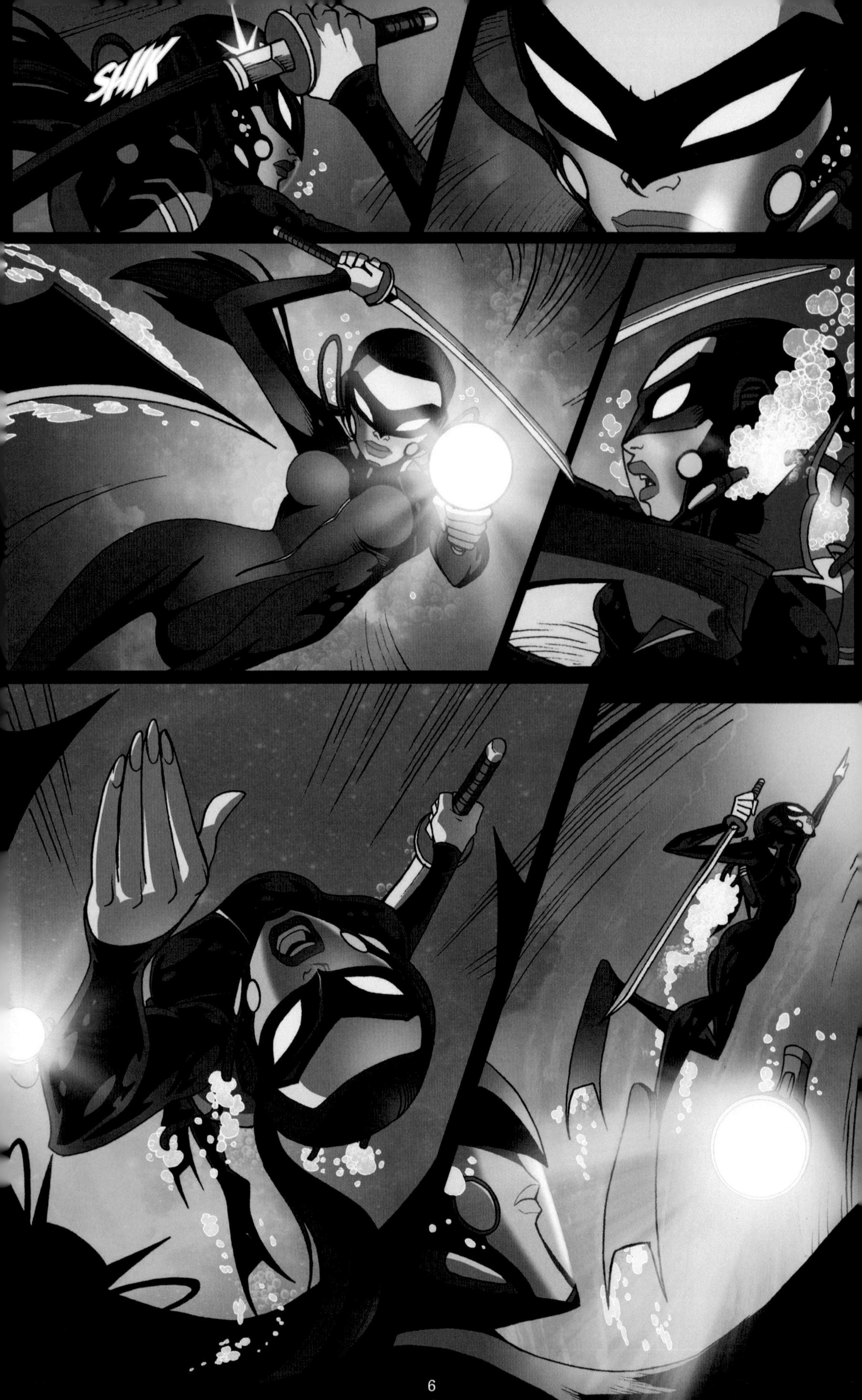
SHIK

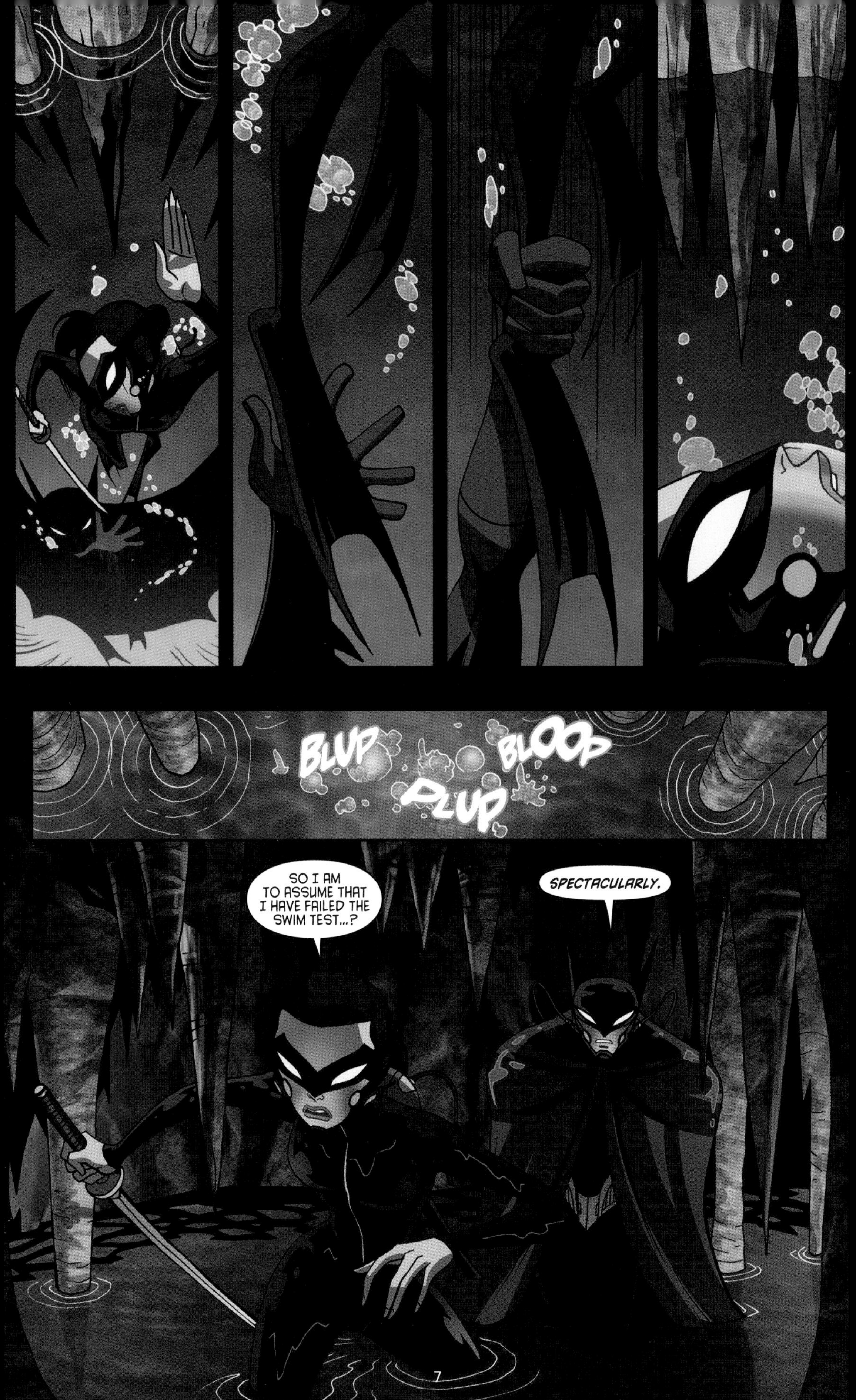
BLUP
PLUP
BLOOP
SO I AM TO ASSUME THAT I HAVE FAILED THE SWIM TEST...?
SPECTACULARLY.

"Tobias Awaits"

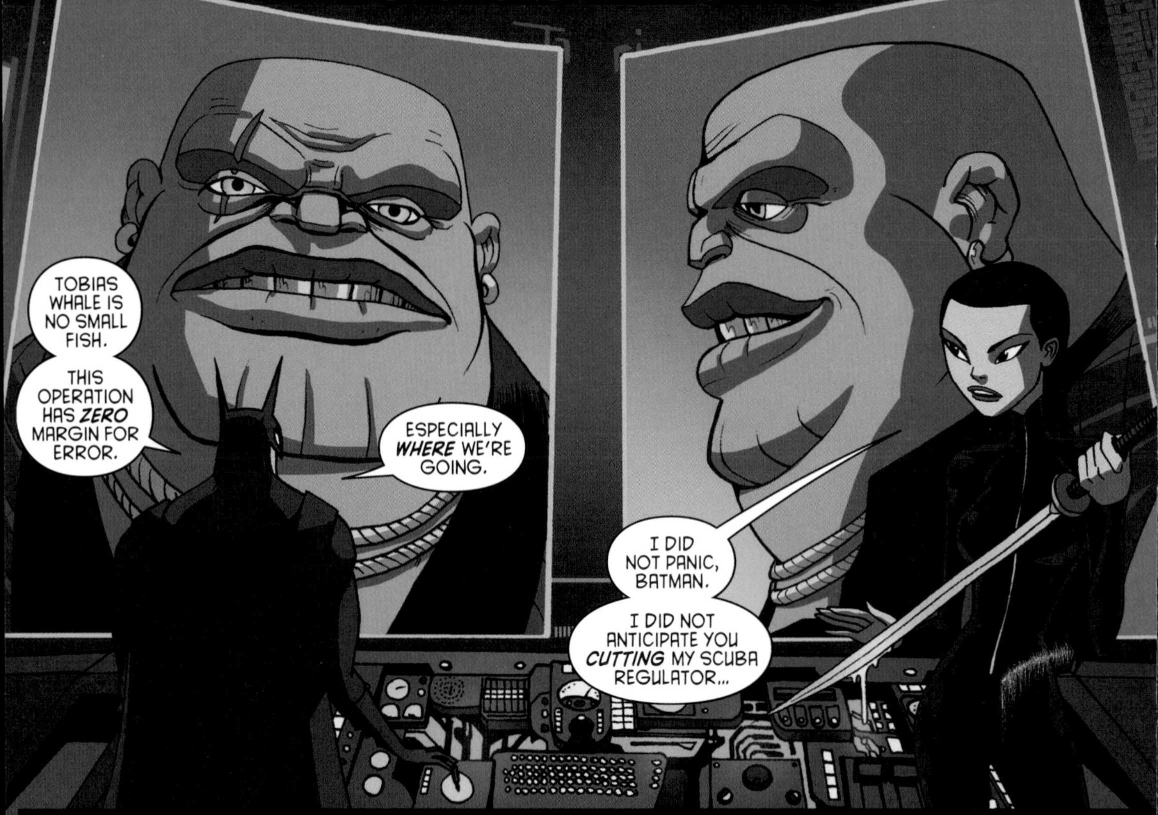
TOBIAS WHALE IS NO SMALL FISH.
THIS OPERATION HAS *ZERO* MARGIN FOR ERROR.
ESPECIALLY *WHERE* WE'RE GOING.
I DID NOT PANIC, BATMAN.
I DID NOT ANTICIPATE YOU *CUTTING* MY SCUBA REGULATOR...

STORY BY **Scott Beatty** ART & COVER BY **Luciano Vecchio** LETTERS BY **Wes Abbott** EDITOR **Alex Antone** BATMAN CREATED BY **Bob Kane**

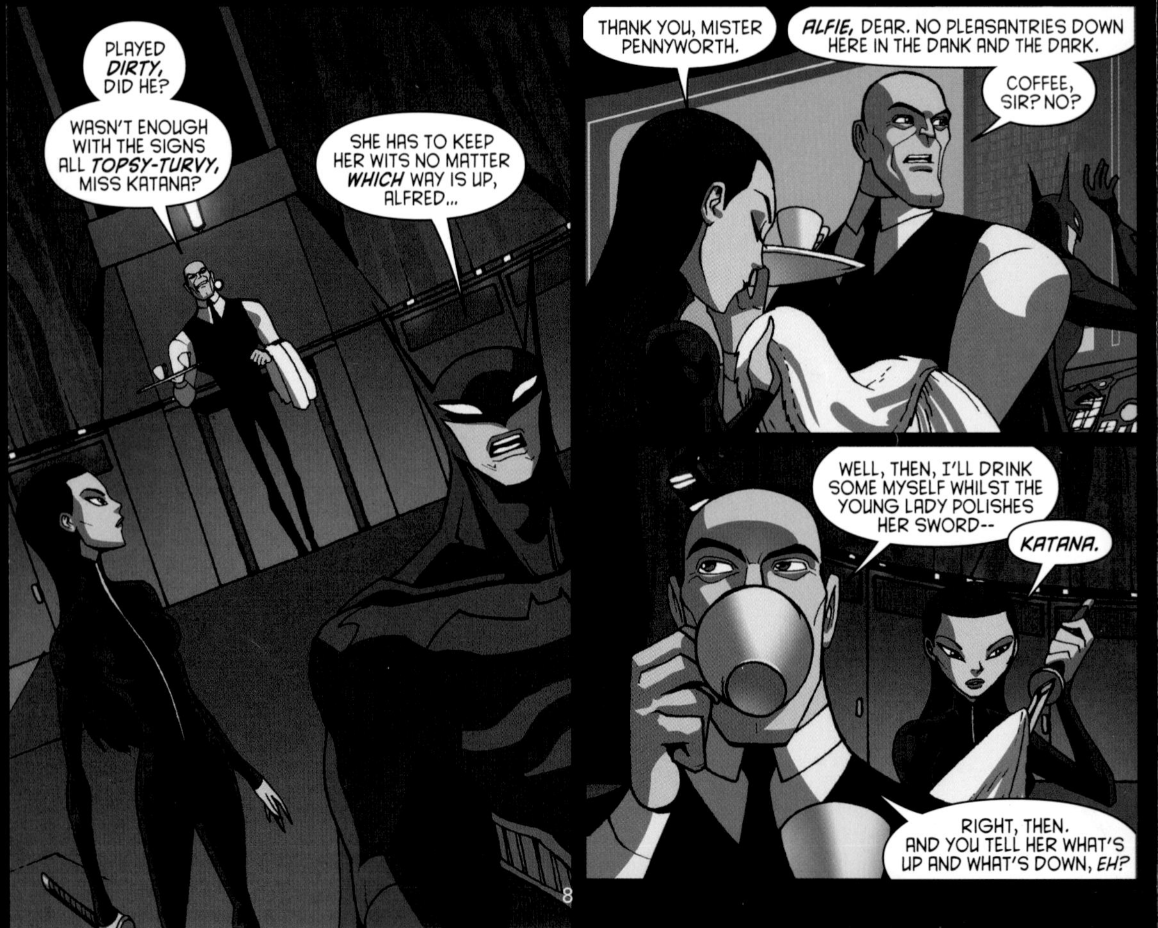
PLAYED *DIRTY*, DID HE?
WASN'T ENOUGH WITH THE SIGNS ALL *TOPSY-TURVY*, MISS KATANA?
SHE HAS TO KEEP HER WITS NO MATTER *WHICH* WAY IS UP, ALFRED...
THANK YOU, MISTER PENNYWORTH.
ALFIE, DEAR. NO PLEASANTRIES DOWN HERE IN THE DANK AND THE DARK.
COFFEE, SIR? NO?
WELL, THEN, I'LL DRINK SOME MYSELF WHILST THE YOUNG LADY POLISHES HER SWORD--
KATANA.
RIGHT, THEN. AND YOU TELL HER WHAT'S UP AND WHAT'S DOWN, *EH?*

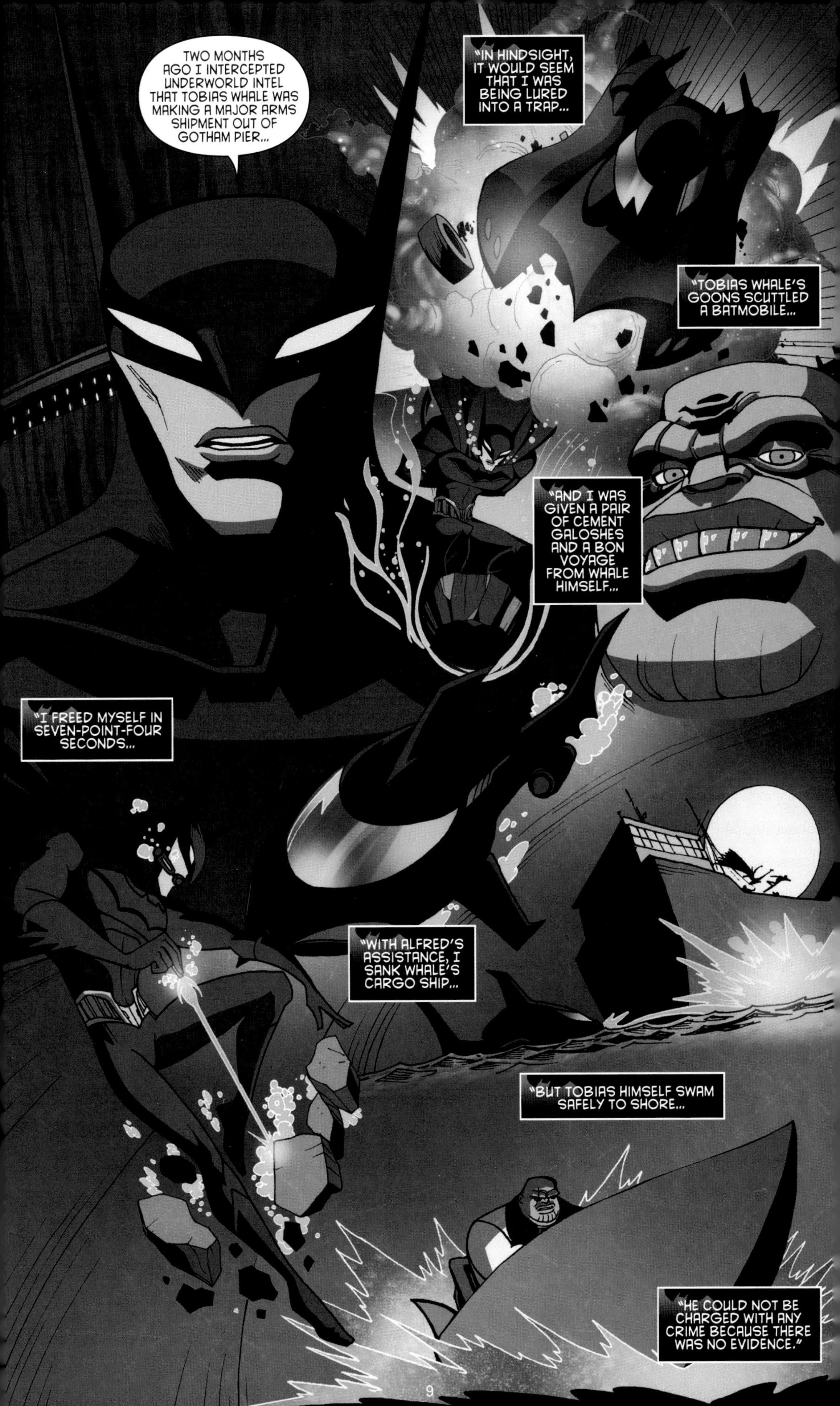
TWO MONTHS AGO I INTERCEPTED UNDERWORLD INTEL THAT TOBIAS WHALE WAS MAKING A MAJOR ARMS SHIPMENT OUT OF GOTHAM PIER...
"IN HINDSIGHT, IT WOULD SEEM THAT I WAS BEING LURED INTO A TRAP...
"TOBIAS WHALE'S GOONS SCUTTLED A BATMOBILE...
"AND I WAS GIVEN A PAIR OF CEMENT GALOSHES AND A BON VOYAGE FROM WHALE HIMSELF...
"I FREED MYSELF IN SEVEN-POINT-FOUR SECONDS...
"WITH ALFRED'S ASSISTANCE, I SANK WHALE'S CARGO SHIP...
"BUT TOBIAS HIMSELF SWAM SAFELY TO SHORE...
"HE COULD NOT BE CHARGED WITH ANY CRIME BECAUSE THERE WAS NO EVIDENCE."

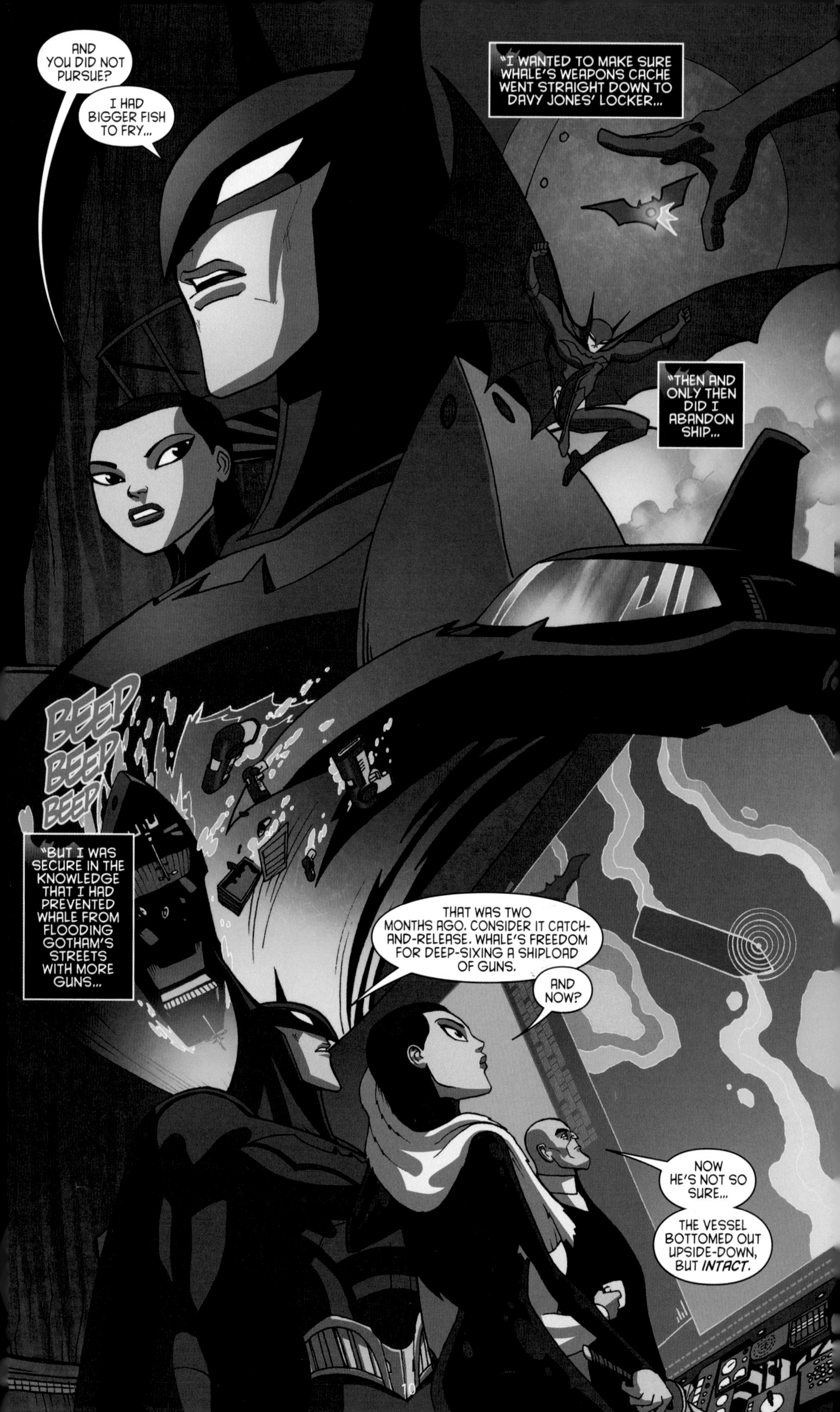
AND YOU DID NOT PURSUE?
I HAD BIGGER FISH TO FRY...
"I WANTED TO MAKE SURE WHALE'S WEAPONS CACHE WENT STRAIGHT DOWN TO DAVY JONES' LOCKER...
"THEN AND ONLY THEN DID I ABANDON SHIP...
BEEP BEEP BEEP
"BUT I WAS SECURE IN THE KNOWLEDGE THAT I HAD PREVENTED WHALE FROM FLOODING GOTHAM'S STREETS WITH MORE GUNS...
THAT WAS TWO MONTHS AGO. CONSIDER IT CATCH-AND-RELEASE. WHALE'S FREEDOM FOR DEEP-SIXING A SHIPLOAD OF GUNS.
AND NOW?
NOW HE'S NOT SO SURE...
THE VESSEL BOTTOMED OUT UPSIDE-DOWN, BUT *INTACT*.

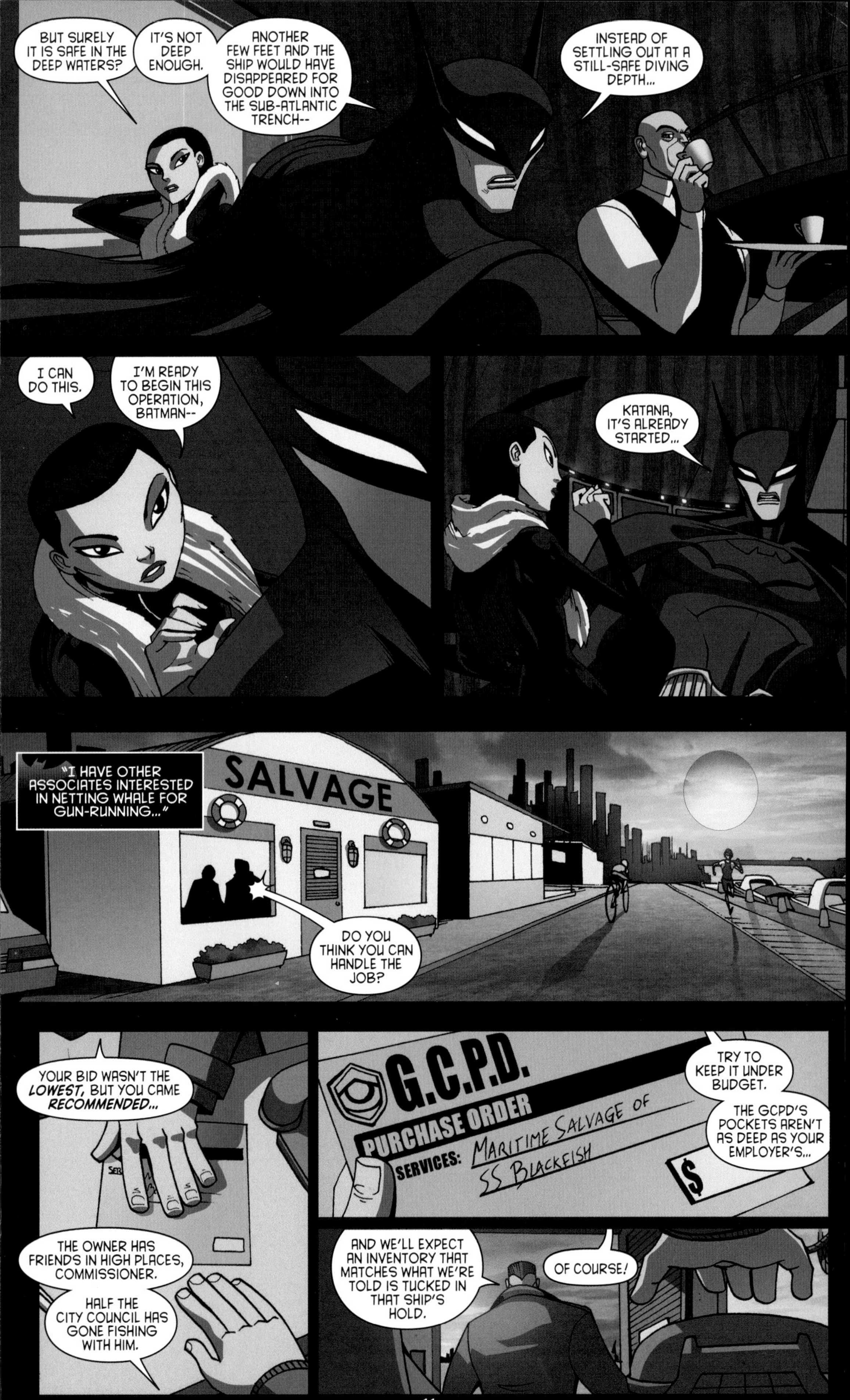

BUT SURELY IT IS SAFE IN THE DEEP WATERS?
IT'S NOT DEEP ENOUGH.
ANOTHER FEW FEET AND THE SHIP WOULD HAVE DISAPPEARED FOR GOOD DOWN INTO THE SUB-ATLANTIC TRENCH--
INSTEAD OF SETTLING OUT AT A STILL-SAFE DIVING DEPTH...
I CAN DO THIS.
I'M READY TO BEGIN THIS OPERATION, BATMAN--
KATANA, IT'S ALREADY STARTED...
"I HAVE OTHER ASSOCIATES INTERESTED IN NETTING WHALE FOR GUN-RUNNING..."
SALVAGE
DO YOU THINK YOU CAN HANDLE THE JOB?
YOUR BID WASN'T THE *LOWEST,* BUT YOU CAME *RECOMMENDED...*
G.C.P.D.
PURCHASE ORDER
SERVICES: MARITIME SALVAGE OF SS BLACKFISH
$
TRY TO KEEP IT UNDER BUDGET.
THE GCPD'S POCKETS AREN'T AS DEEP AS YOUR EMPLOYER'S...
THE OWNER HAS FRIENDS IN HIGH PLACES, COMMISSIONER.
HALF THE CITY COUNCIL HAS GONE FISHING WITH HIM.
AND WE'LL EXPECT AN INVENTORY THAT MATCHES WHAT WE'RE TOLD IS TUCKED IN THAT SHIP'S HOLD.
OF COURSE!

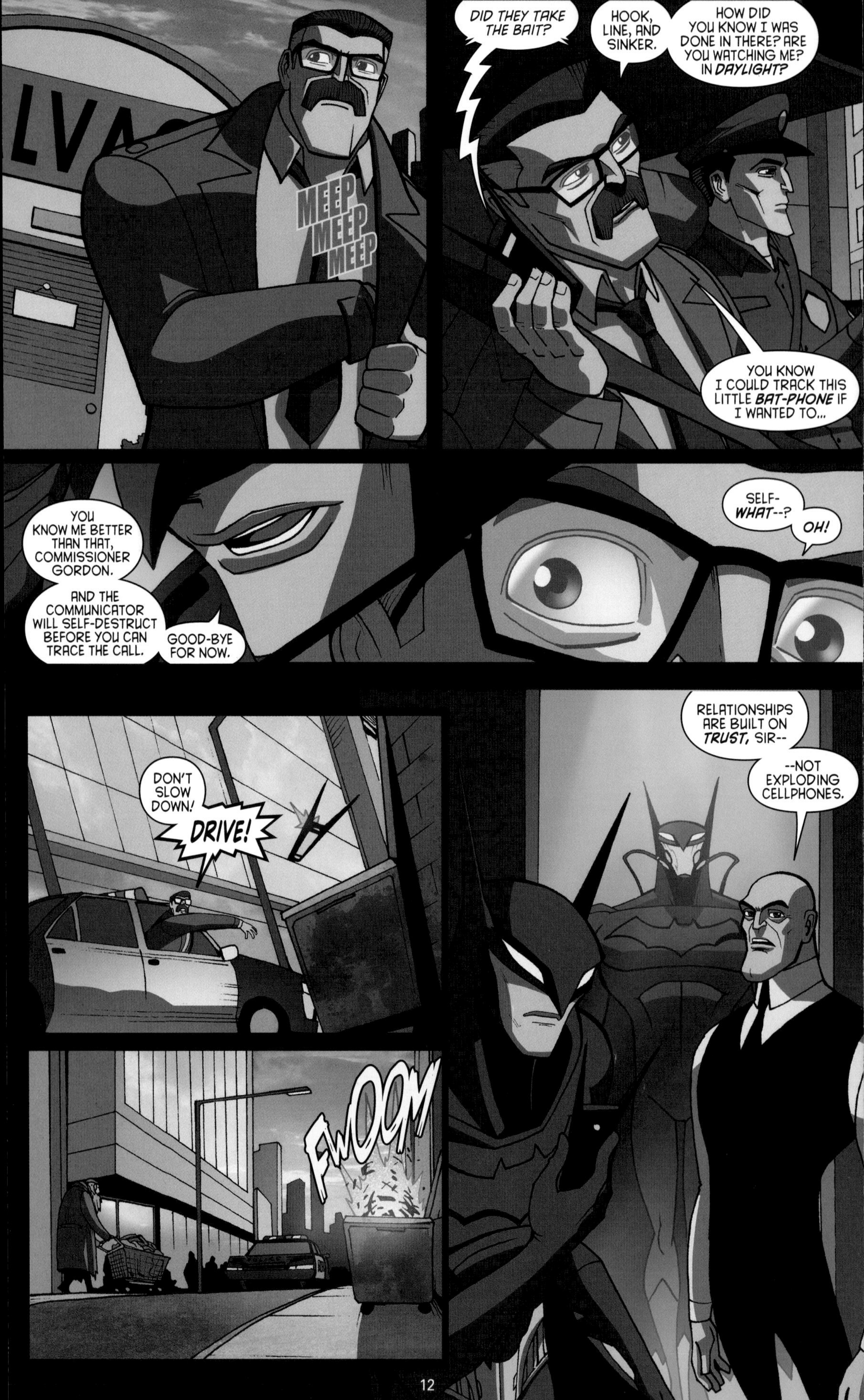
MEEP MEEP MEEP
DID THEY TAKE THE BAIT?
HOOK, LINE, AND SINKER.
HOW DID YOU KNOW I WAS DONE IN THERE? ARE YOU WATCHING ME? IN DAYLIGHT?
YOU KNOW I COULD TRACK THIS LITTLE BAT-PHONE IF I WANTED TO...
YOU KNOW ME BETTER THAN THAT, COMMISSIONER GORDON.
AND THE COMMUNICATOR WILL SELF-DESTRUCT BEFORE YOU CAN TRACE THE CALL.
GOOD-BYE FOR NOW.
SELF-WHAT--?
OH!
DON'T SLOW DOWN!
DRIVE!
FWOOM
RELATIONSHIPS ARE BUILT ON TRUST, SIR--
--NOT EXPLODING CELLPHONES.

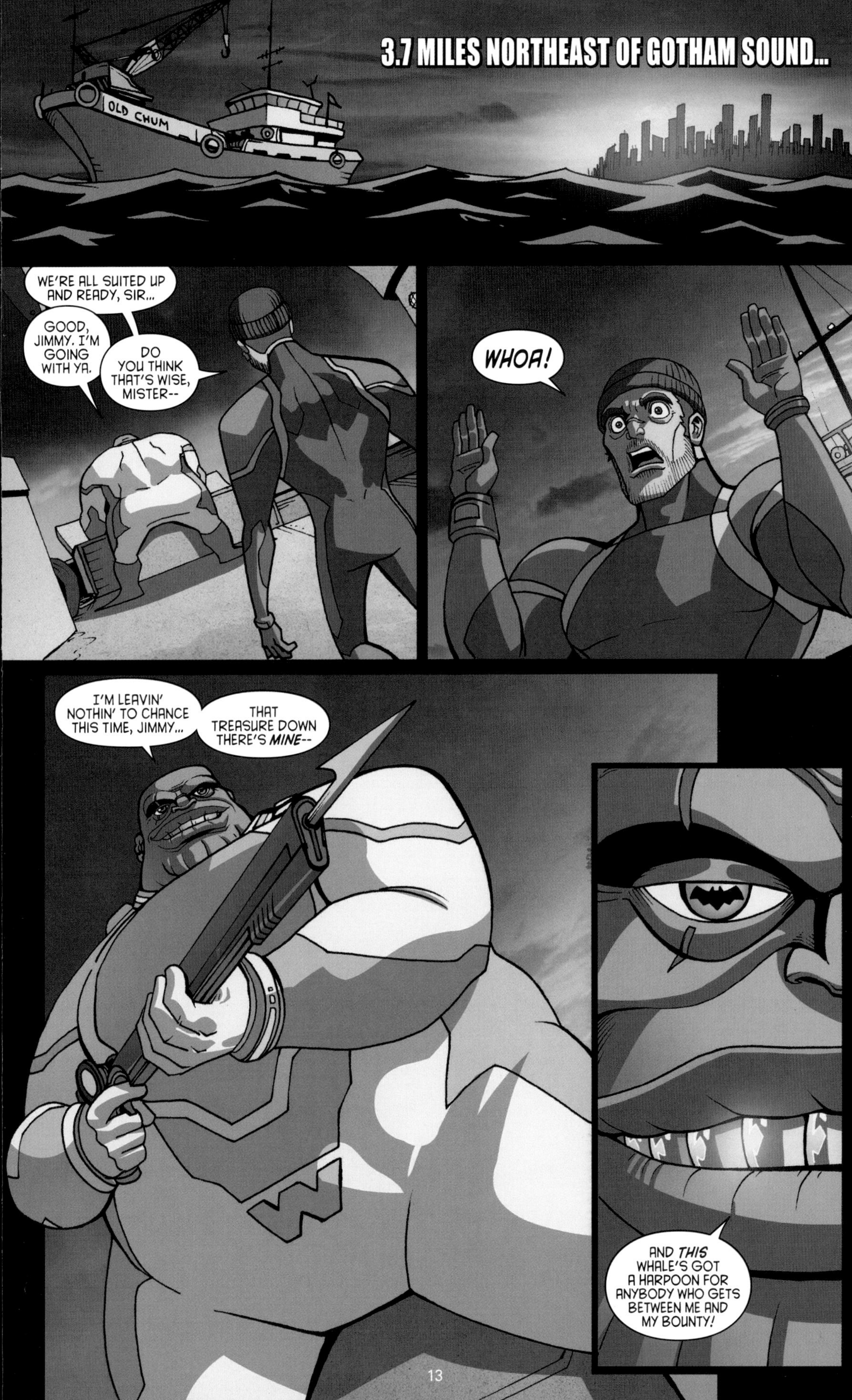
3.7 MILES NORTHEAST OF GOTHAM SOUND...
OLD CHUM
WE'RE ALL SUITED UP AND READY, SIR...
GOOD, JIMMY. I'M GOING WITH YA.
DO YOU THINK THAT'S WISE, MISTER--
WHOA!
I'M LEAVIN' NOTHIN' TO CHANCE THIS TIME, JIMMY...
THAT TREASURE DOWN THERE'S *MINE*--
AND *THIS* WHALE'S GOT A HARPOON FOR ANYBODY WHO GETS BETWEEN ME AND MY BOUNTY!

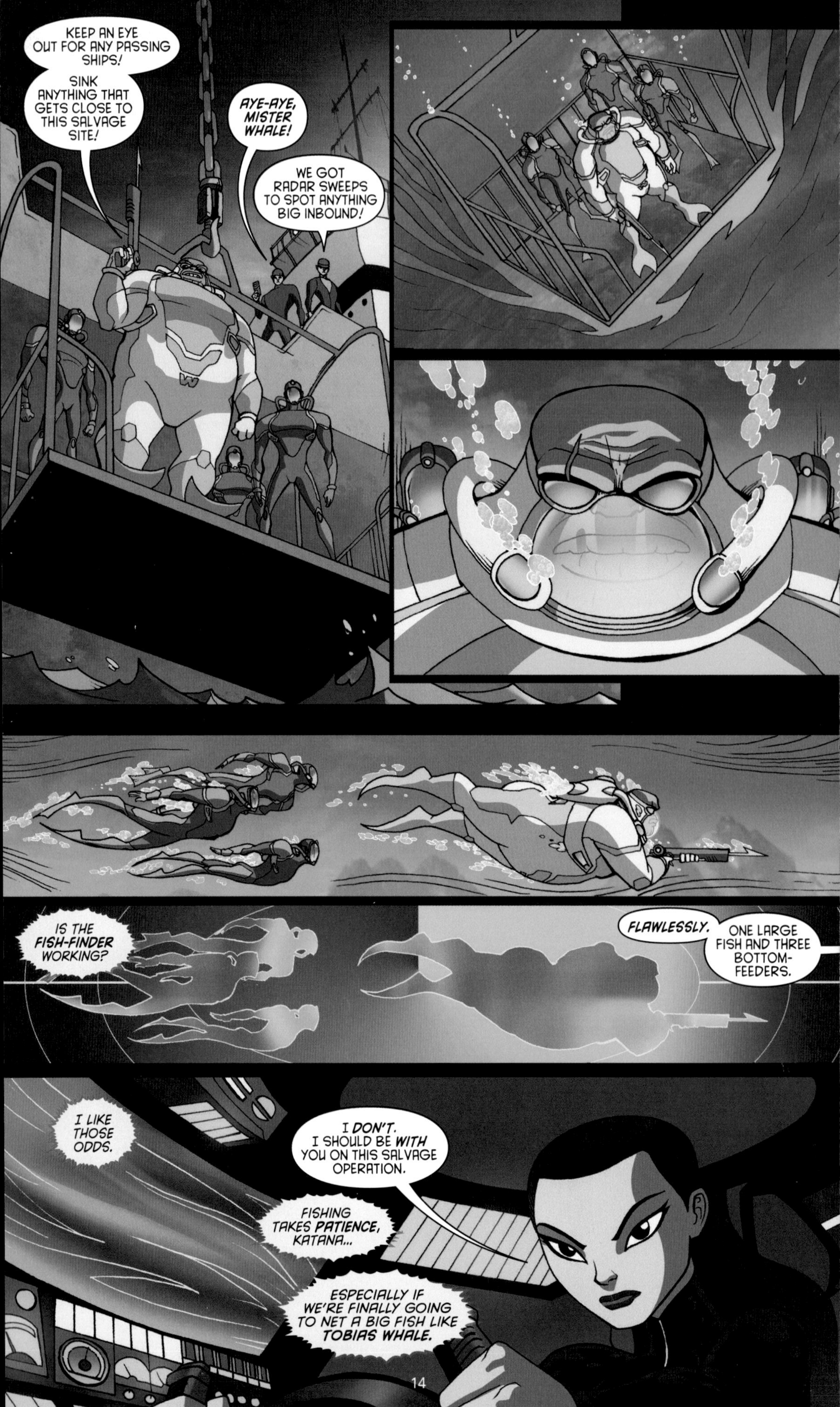

KEEP AN EYE OUT FOR ANY PASSING SHIPS!
SINK ANYTHING THAT GETS CLOSE TO THIS SALVAGE SITE!
AYE-AYE, MISTER WHALE!
WE GOT RADAR SWEEPS TO SPOT ANYTHING BIG INBOUND!
IS THE FISH-FINDER WORKING?
FLAWLESSLY.
ONE LARGE FISH AND THREE BOTTOM-FEEDERS.
I LIKE THOSE ODDS.
I DON'T. I SHOULD BE WITH YOU ON THIS SALVAGE OPERATION.
FISHING TAKES PATIENCE, KATANA...
ESPECIALLY IF WE'RE FINALLY GOING TO NET A BIG FISH LIKE TOBIAS WHALE.

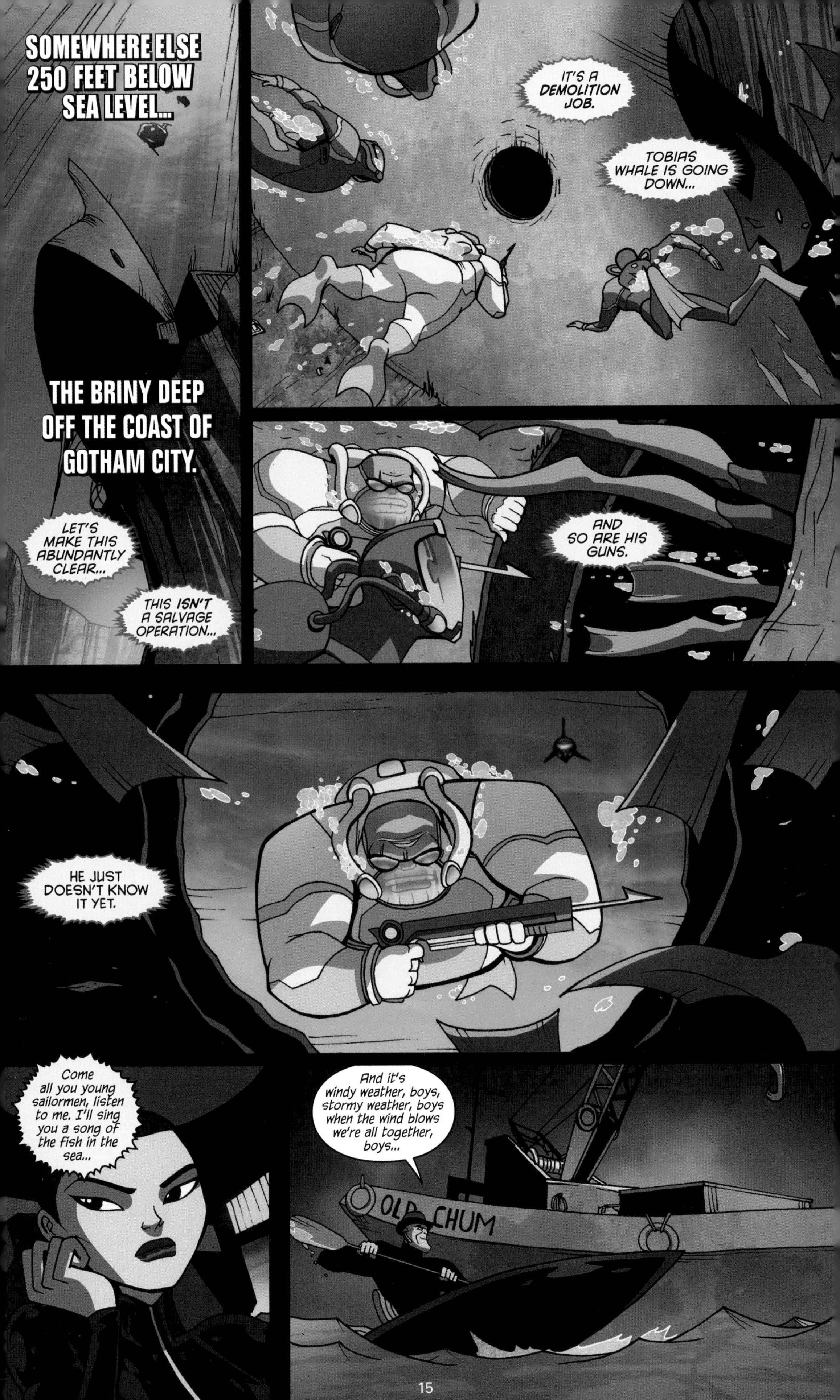
SOMEWHERE ELSE 250 FEET BELOW SEA LEVEL...
IT'S A DEMOLITION JOB.
TOBIAS WHALE IS GOING DOWN...
THE BRINY DEEP OFF THE COAST OF GOTHAM CITY.
LET'S MAKE THIS ABUNDANTLY CLEAR...
THIS ISN'T A SALVAGE OPERATION...
AND SO ARE HIS GUNS.
HE JUST DOESN'T KNOW IT YET.
Come all you young sailormen, listen to me. I'll sing you a song of the fish in the sea...
And it's windy weather, boys, stormy weather, boys when the wind blows we're all together, boys...
OLD CHUM

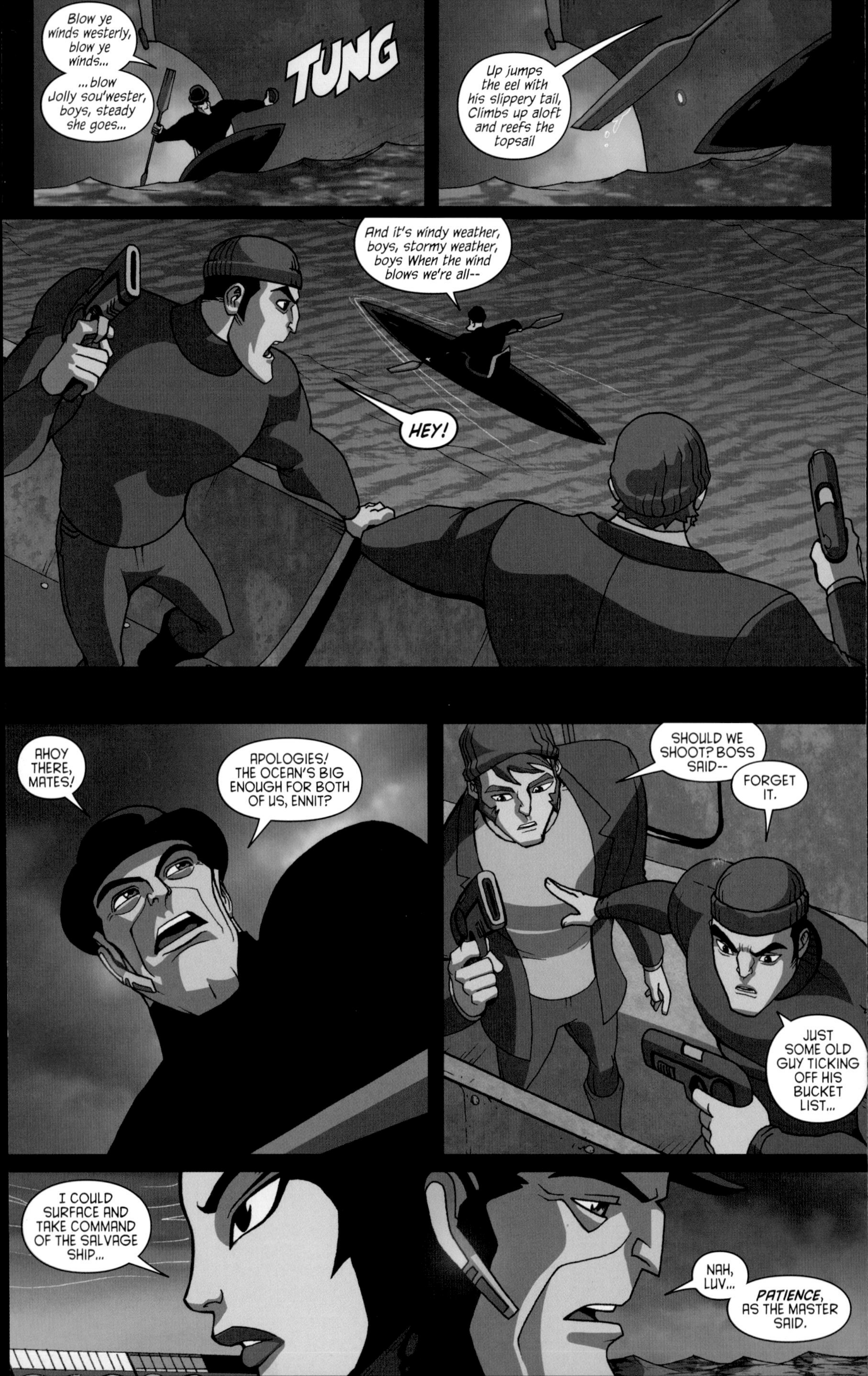
Blow ye winds westerly, blow ye winds...
...blow Jolly sou'wester, boys, steady she goes...
TUNG
Up jumps the eel with his slippery tail, Climbs up aloft and reefs the topsail
And it's windy weather, boys, stormy weather, boys When the wind blows we're all--
HEY!
AHOY THERE, MATES!
APOLOGIES! THE OCEAN'S BIG ENOUGH FOR BOTH OF US, ENNIT?
SHOULD WE SHOOT? BOSS SAID--
FORGET IT.
JUST SOME OLD GUY TICKING OFF HIS BUCKET LIST...
I COULD SURFACE AND TAKE COMMAND OF THE SALVAGE SHIP...
NAH, LUV...
PATIENCE, AS THE MASTER SAID.

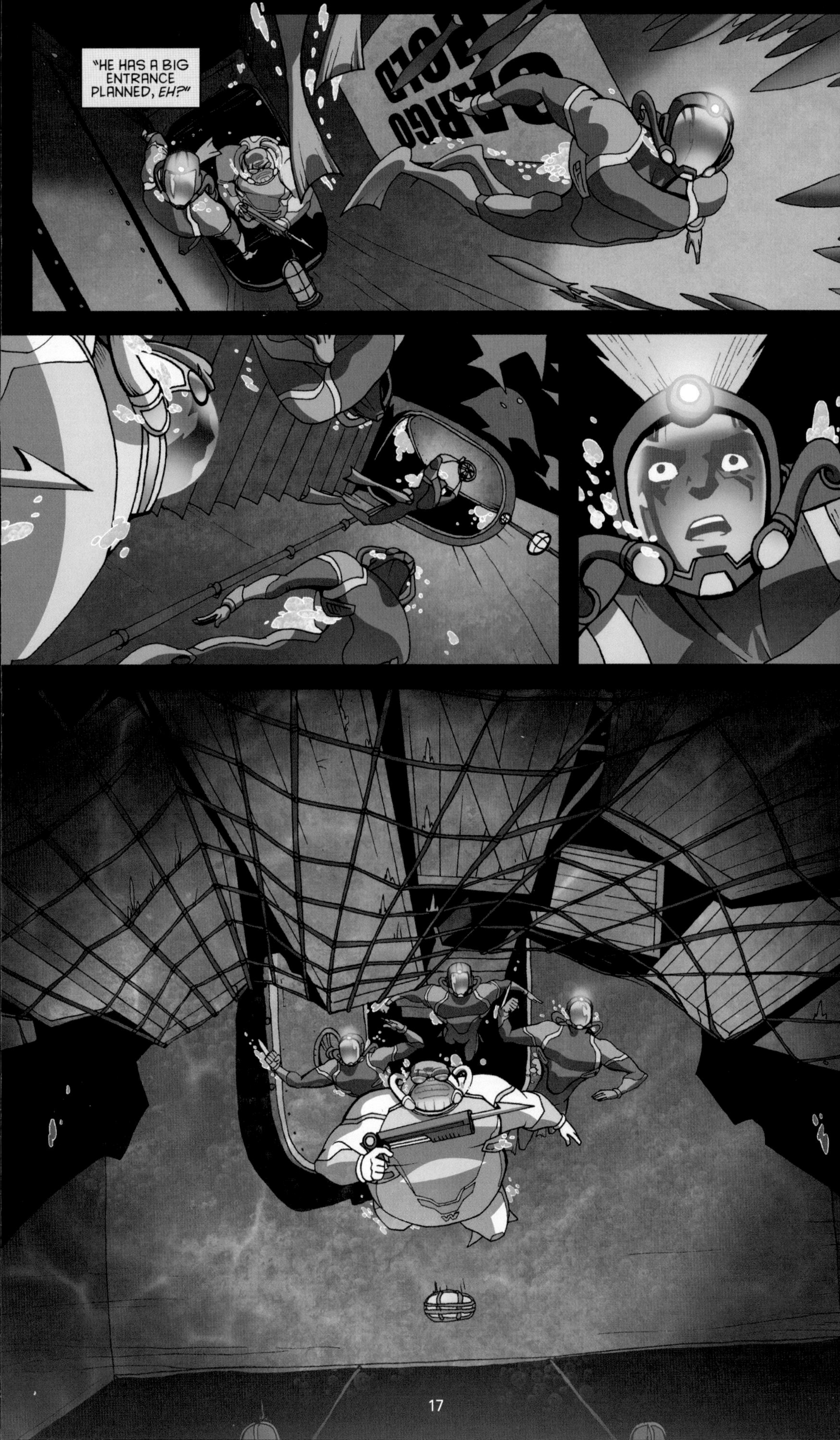
"HE HAS A BIG ENTRANCE PLANNED, EH?"

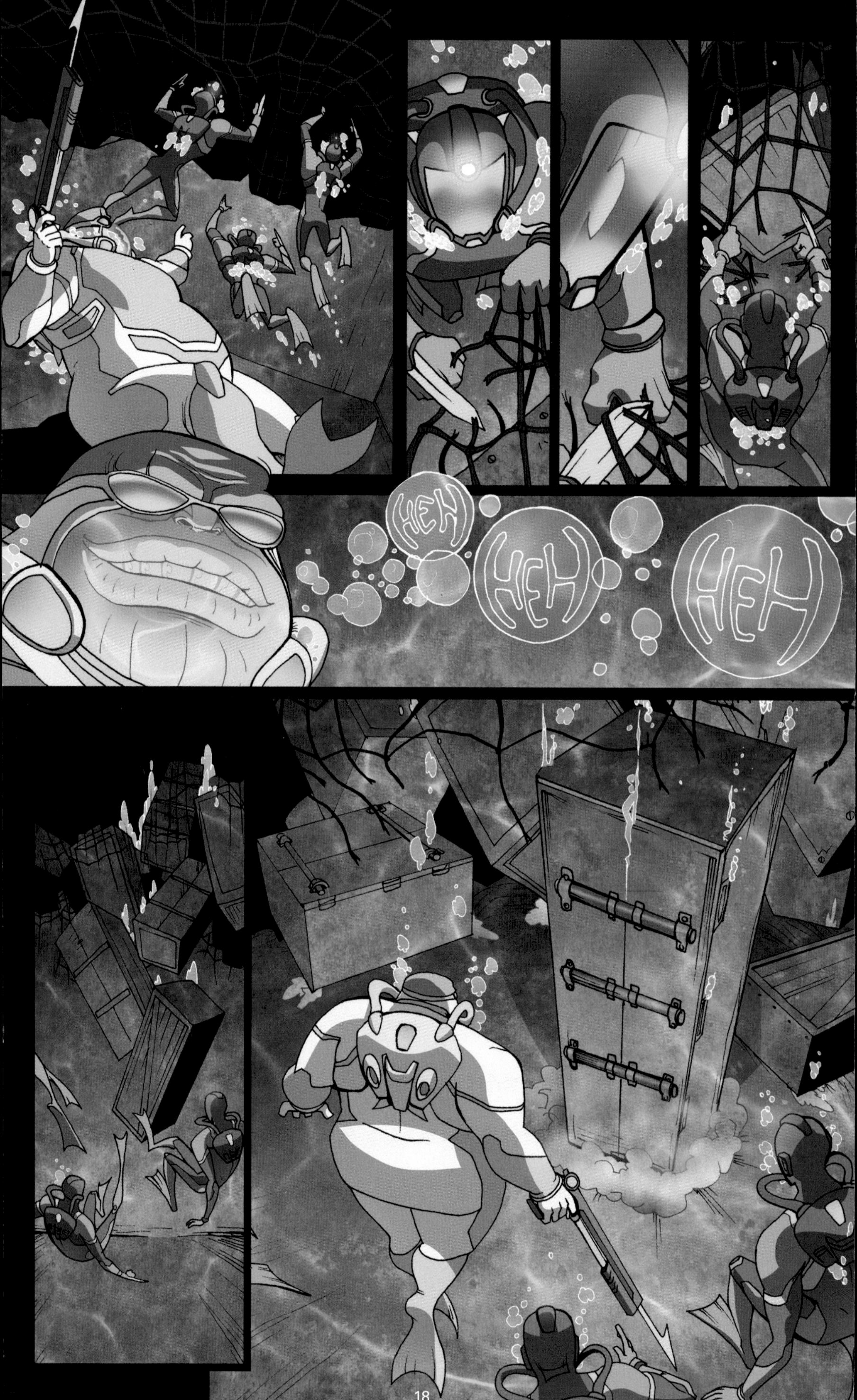
HEH
HEH
HEH

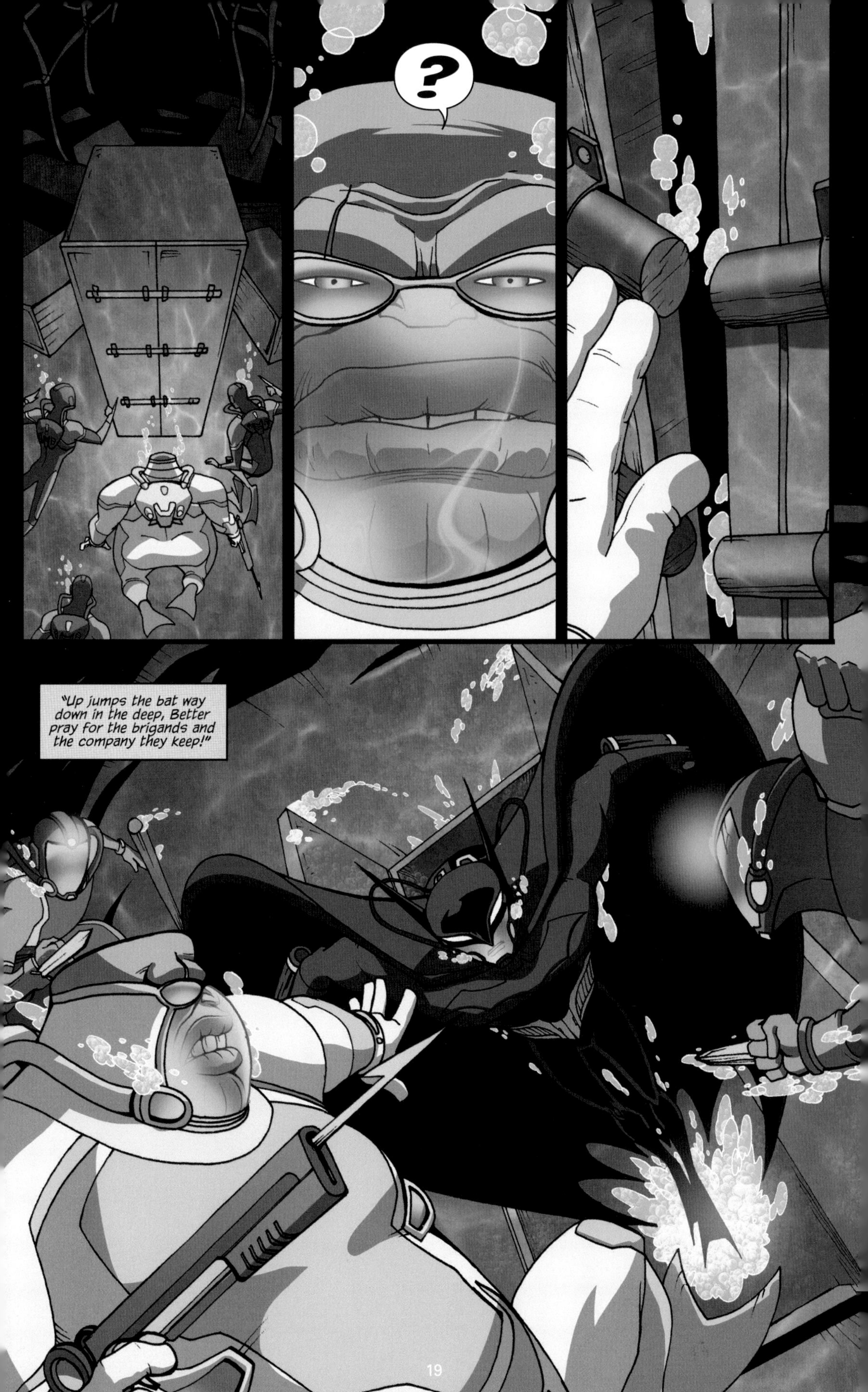
?
"Up jumps the bat way down in the deep, Better pray for the brigands and the company they keep!"

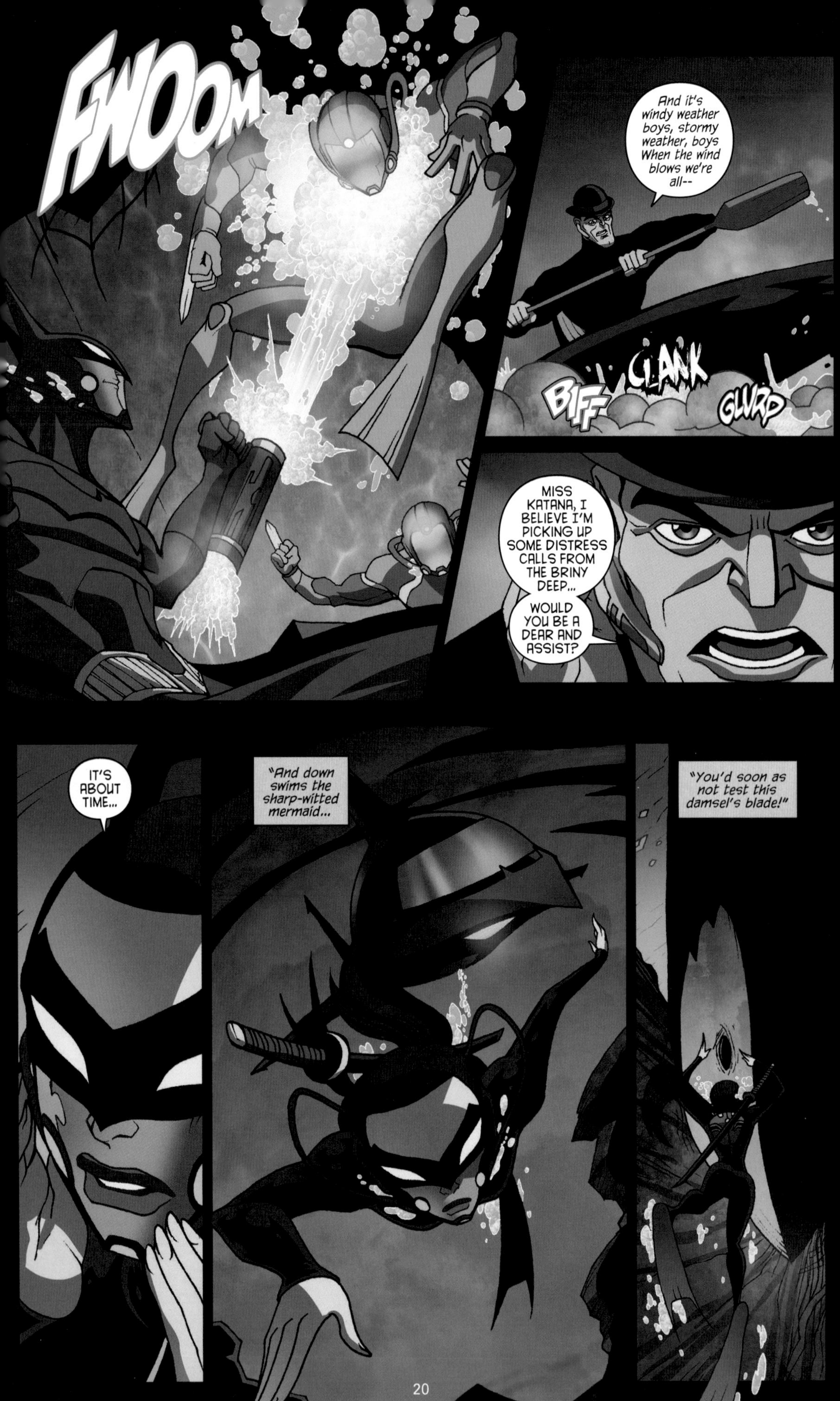
FWOOM
And it's windy weather boys, stormy weather, boys When the wind blows we're all--
BIFF
CLANK
GLURP
MISS KATANA, I BELIEVE I'M PICKING UP SOME DISTRESS CALLS FROM THE BRINY DEEP...
WOULD YOU BE A DEAR AND ASSIST?
IT'S ABOUT TIME...
"And down swims the sharp-witted mermaid...
"You'd soon as not test this damsel's blade!"

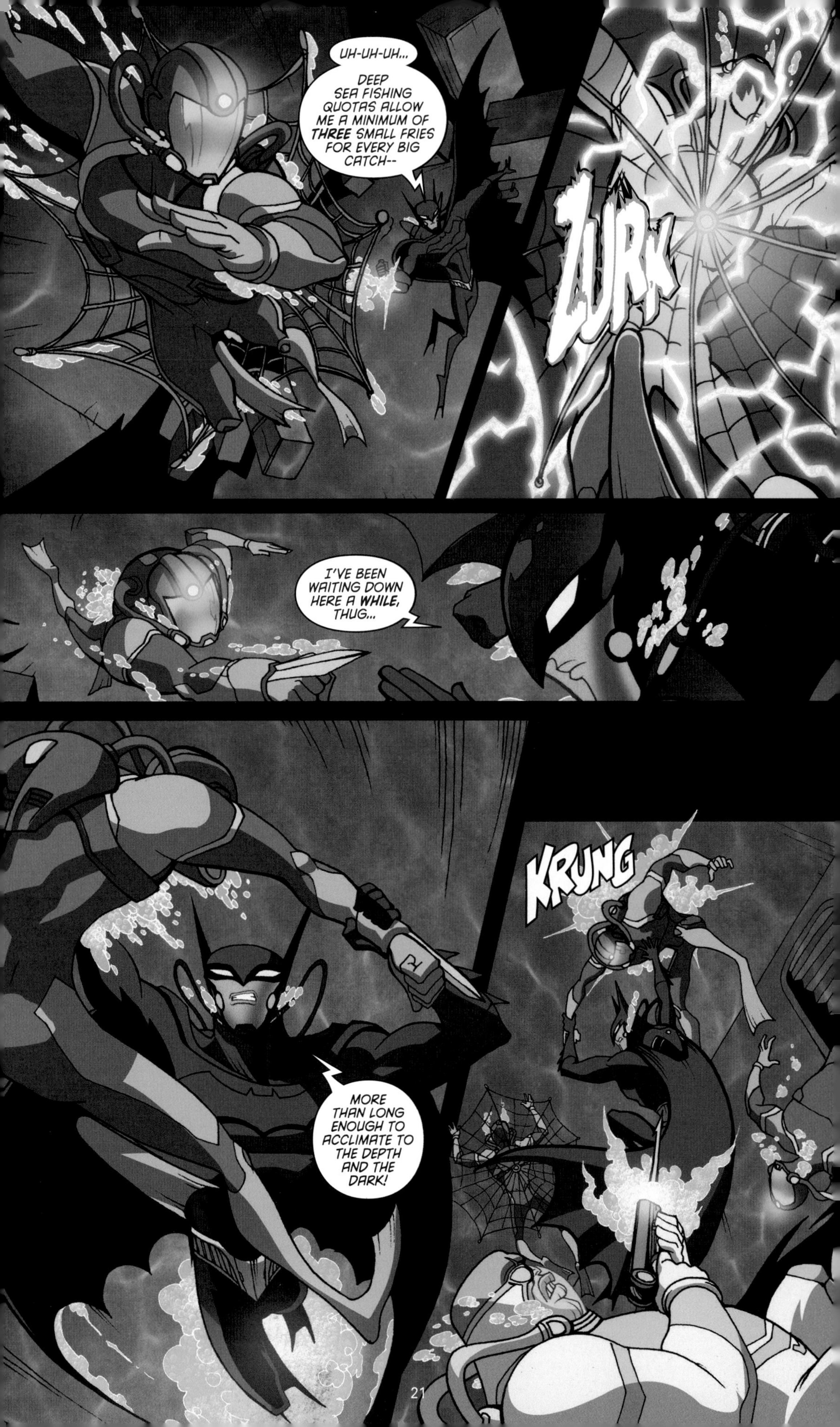
UH-UH-UH... DEEP SEA FISHING QUOTAS ALLOW ME A MINIMUM OF THREE SMALL FRIES FOR EVERY BIG CATCH--
ZURK
I'VE BEEN WAITING DOWN HERE A WHILE, THUG...
MORE THAN LONG ENOUGH TO ACCLIMATE TO THE DEPTH AND THE DARK!
KRUNG

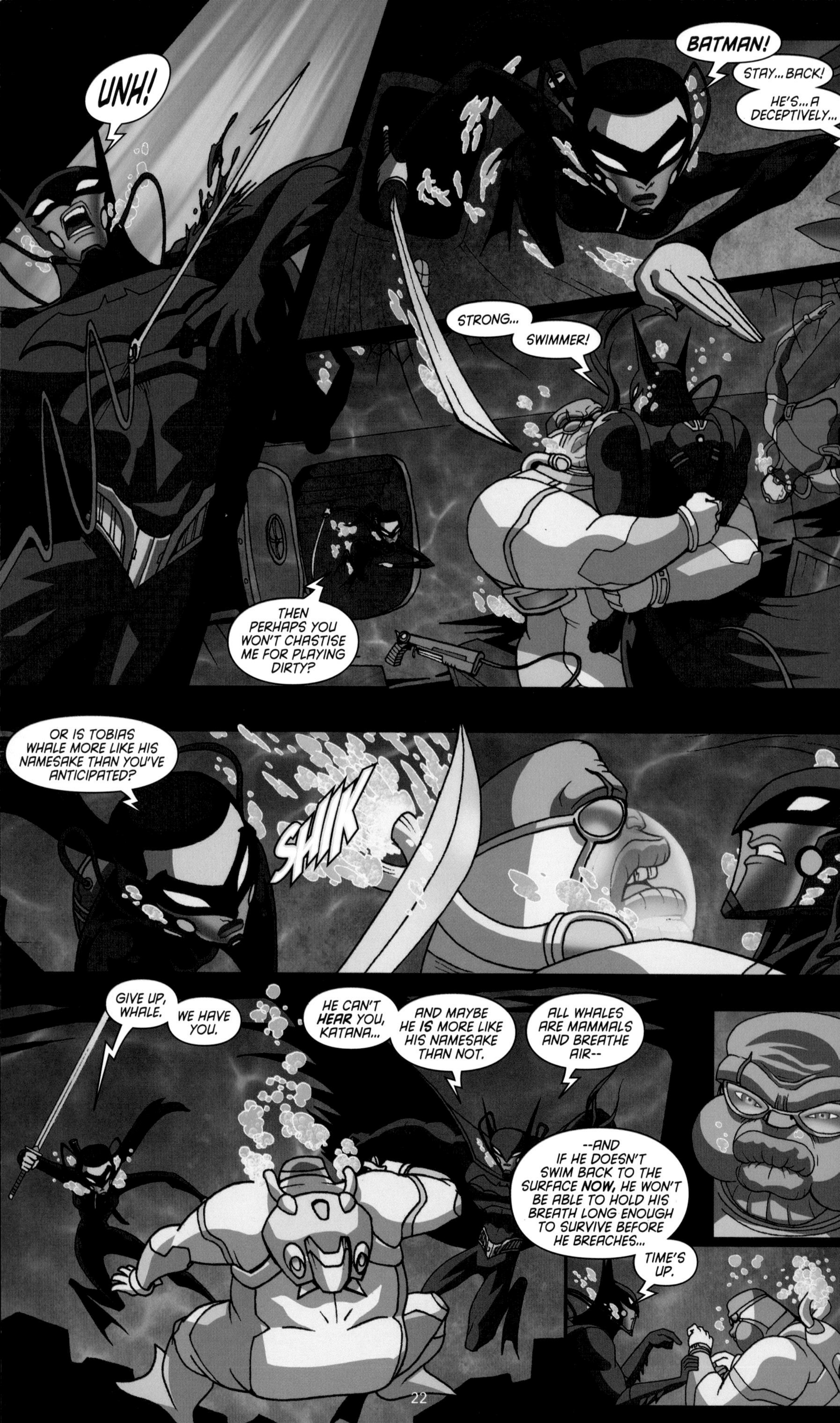
UNH!
BATMAN!
STAY... BACK!
HE'S... A DECEPTIVELY...
STRONG...
SWIMMER!
THEN PERHAPS YOU WON'T CHASTISE ME FOR PLAYING DIRTY?
OR IS TOBIAS WHALE MORE LIKE HIS NAMESAKE THAN YOU'VE ANTICIPATED?
SHIK
GIVE UP, WHALE.
WE HAVE YOU.
HE CAN'T **HEAR** YOU, KATANA...
AND MAYBE HE **IS** MORE LIKE HIS NAMESAKE THAN NOT.
ALL WHALES ARE MAMMALS AND BREATHE AIR--
--AND IF HE DOESN'T SWIM BACK TO THE SURFACE **NOW,** HE WON'T BE ABLE TO HOLD HIS BREATH LONG ENOUGH TO SURVIVE BEFORE HE BREACHES...
TIME'S UP.

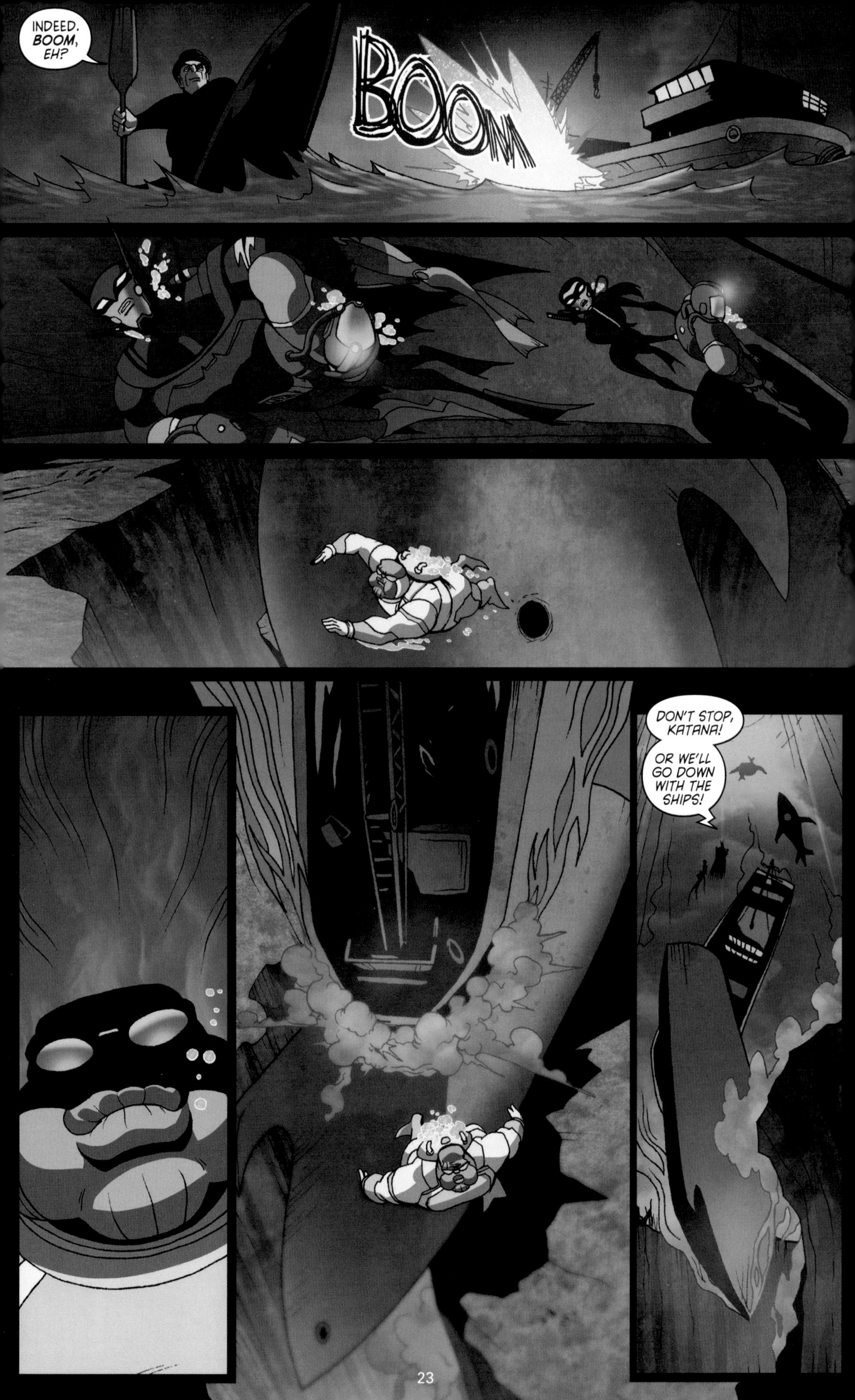
INDEED. BOOM, EH?
BOOOM
DON'T STOP, KATANA!
OR WE'LL GO DOWN WITH THE SHIPS!

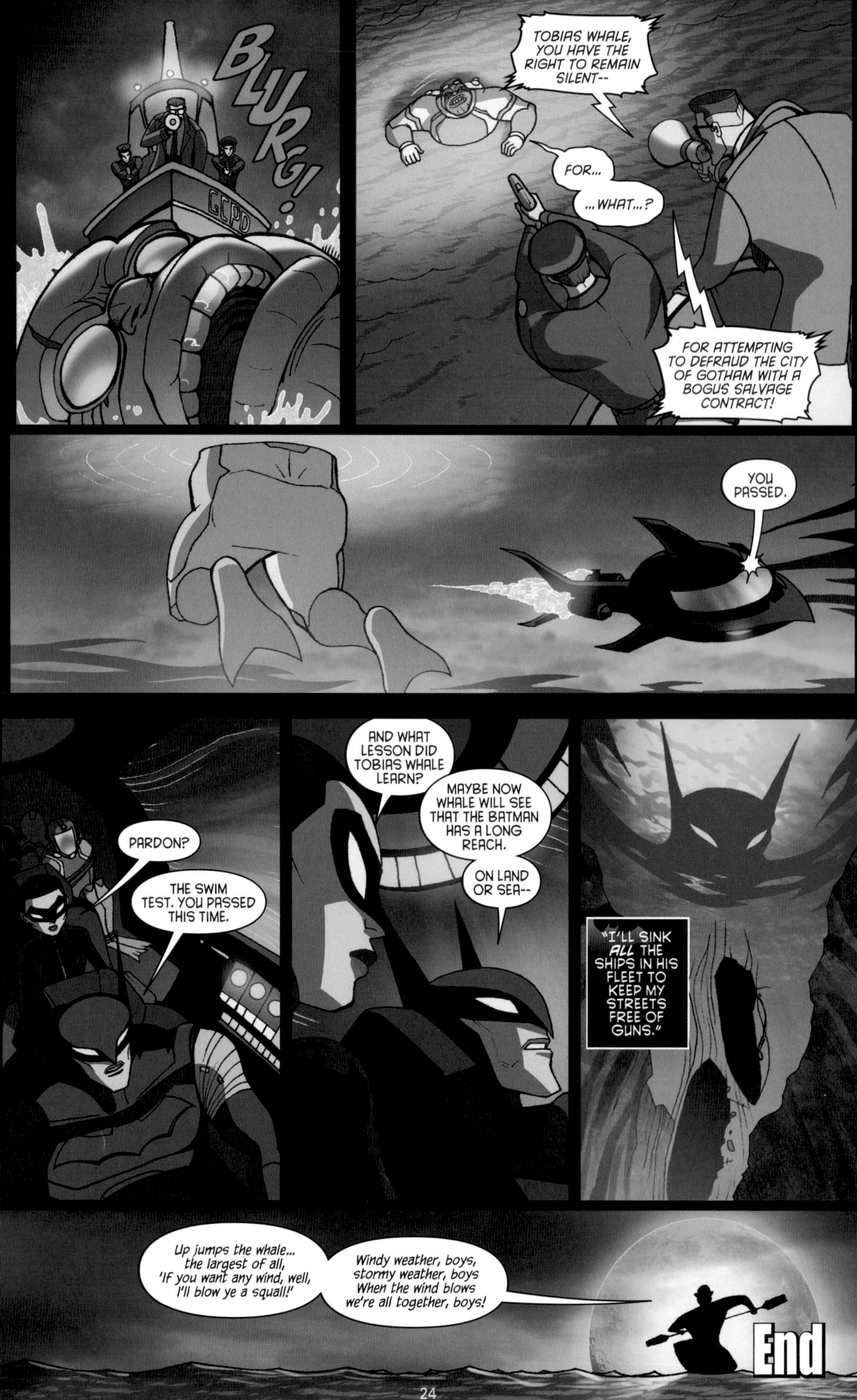
BLURG!
TOBIAS WHALE, YOU HAVE THE RIGHT TO REMAIN SILENT--
FOR...
...WHAT...?
FOR ATTEMPTING TO DEFRAUD THE CITY OF GOTHAM WITH A BOGUS SALVAGE CONTRACT!
YOU PASSED.
PARDON?
THE SWIM TEST. YOU PASSED THIS TIME.
AND WHAT LESSON DID TOBIAS WHALE LEARN?
MAYBE NOW WHALE WILL SEE THAT THE BATMAN HAS A LONG REACH.
ON LAND OR SEA--
"I'LL SINK ALL THE SHIPS IN HIS FLEET TO KEEP MY STREETS FREE OF GUNS."
Up jumps the whale... the largest of all, 'If you want any wind, well, I'll blow ye a squall!'
Windy weather, boys, stormy weather, boys When the wind blows we're all together, boys!
End

CREATORS

SCOTT BEATTY - WRITER

Scott Beatty is the author of many Bat-Books, including *The Batman Handbook,* which is the definitive guide on how to fight crime like the Caped Crusader. He is also the writer of many Bat-Tales for DC Comics, including co-scripting the best-selling *Robin: Year One, Batgirl: Year One,* and *Nightwing: Year One* mini-series. Scott lives in Pennsylvania with his wife Jennifer, their children Finnegan and Hopey, and a stalwart Bernese Mountain Dog named Oscar.

LUCIANO VECCHIO - ILLUSTRATOR

Luciano Vecchio currently lives in Buenos Aires, Argentina. With experience in illustration, animation, and comics, his works have been published in the US, Spain, the UK, France, and Argentina. His credits include Ben 10 [DC Comics], Cruel Thing [Norma], Unseen Tribe [Zuda Comics], Sentinels [Drumfish Productions], and several DC Super Heroes books for Stone Arch Books.

GLOSSARY

abundant [a·BUHN·duhnt·]--existing or occurring in large amounts

anticipate [an·TISS·uh·payt]--to look forward to something, or to predict that something is going to happen

brigands [BRIG·uhndz]--robbers who travel in a group

cache [KASH]--a group of things that have been hidden in a secret place. Also, a part of a computer's memory where information is kept so that the computer can find it very quickly.

chastise [CHASS·tahyz]--to criticize someone harshly for doing something wrong

chum [CHUHM]--a close friend. Also, pieces of fish thrown off a boat as bait to attract other fish, like sharks.

defraud [di·FRAHD]--to trick or cheat someone or something in order to get money

salvage [SAL·vij]--something that is saved from a wreck or fire

scuttled [SKUH·tuhld]--sunk by putting holes in the bottoms or sides

squall [SKWALL]--a sudden and violent wind or storm, particularly at sea

VISUAL QUESTIONS & PROMPTS

1. Why do you think Katana thinks she failed the swim test? What did she do wrong? How could she have passed?

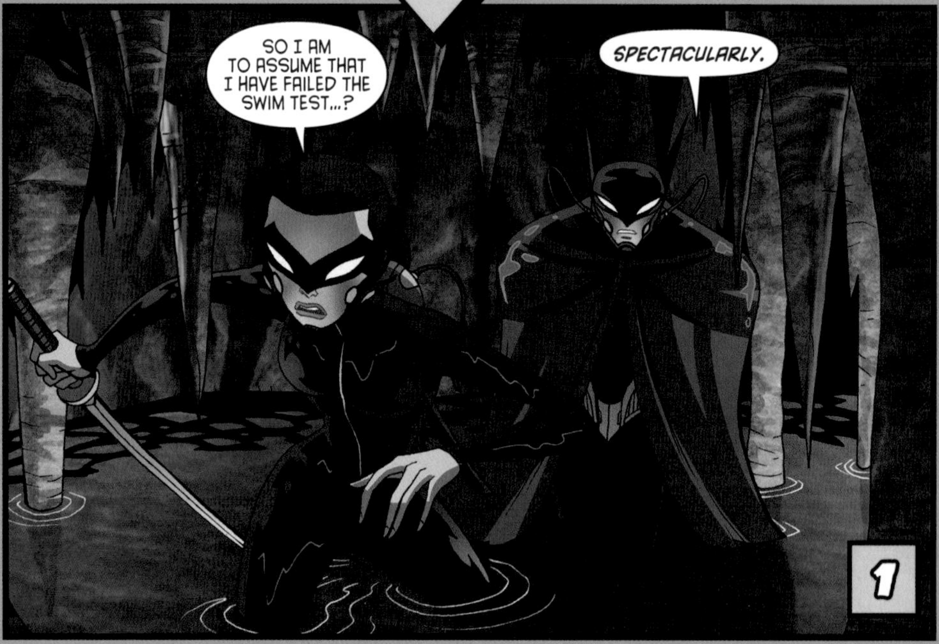
SO I AM TO ASSUME THAT I HAVE FAILED THE SWIM TEST...?
SPECTACULARLY.
1

2. Why is "Old Chum" a clever name for a boat? Check the glossary for a definition of "chum" if you need hints.

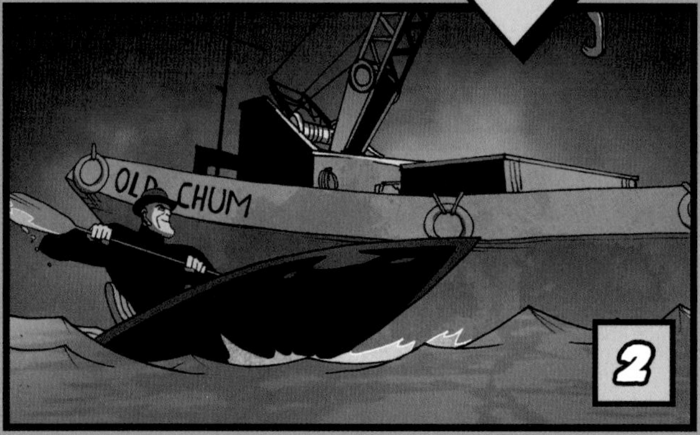
OLD CHUM
2

3. In your own words, describe the sequence of events that happened on page 9 where Batman first encounters Tobias Whale. What happened? How did it turn out?

4. Why did the coloring change between these two panels? Reread page 14 for clues.

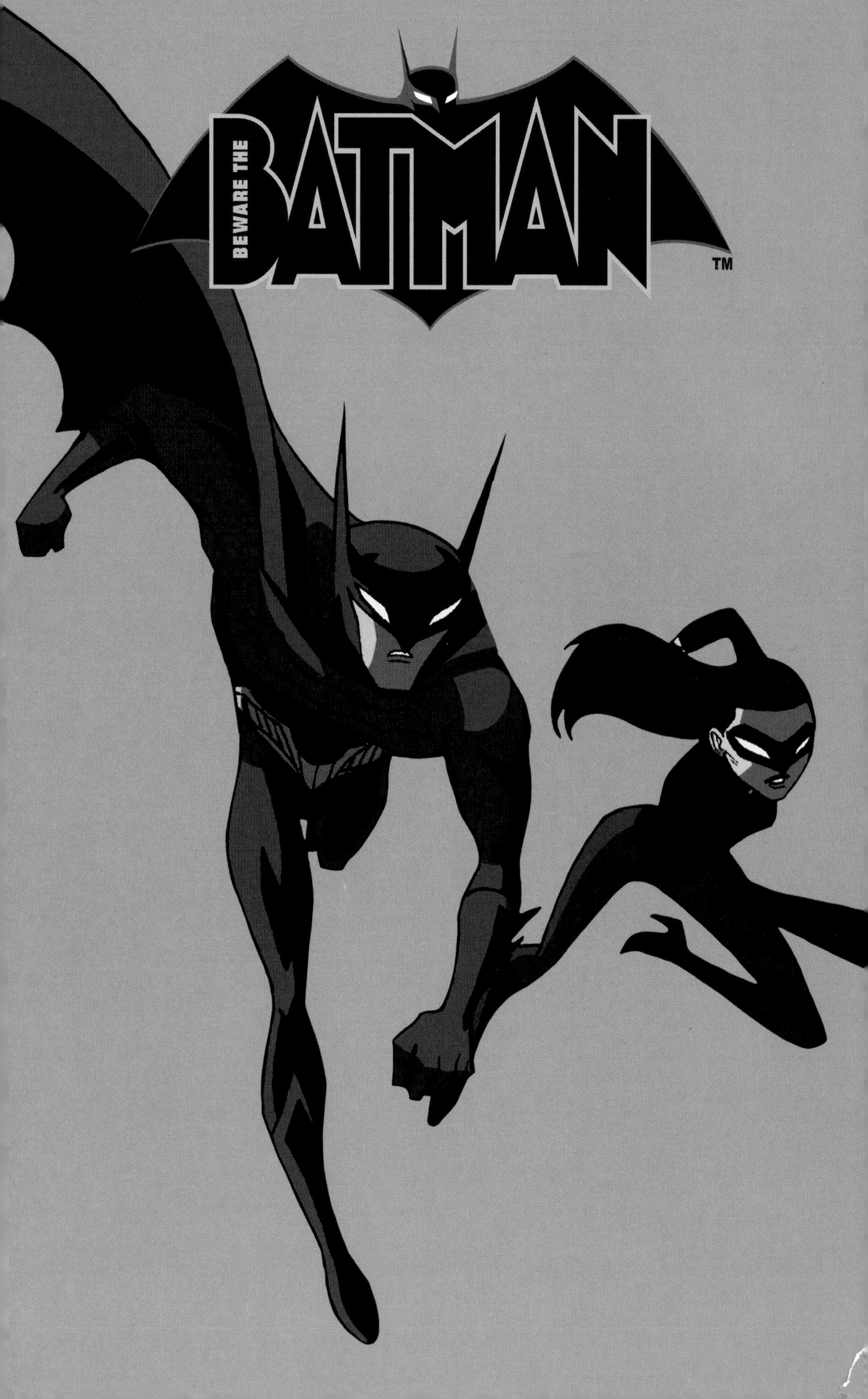
BEWARE THE
BATMAN
TM

READ THEM ALL!

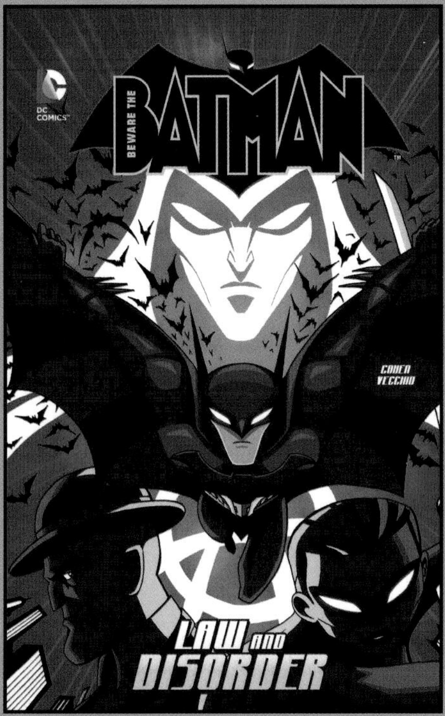
DC COMICS
BEWARE THE
BATMAN
COHEN
VECCHIO
LAW AND
DISORDER

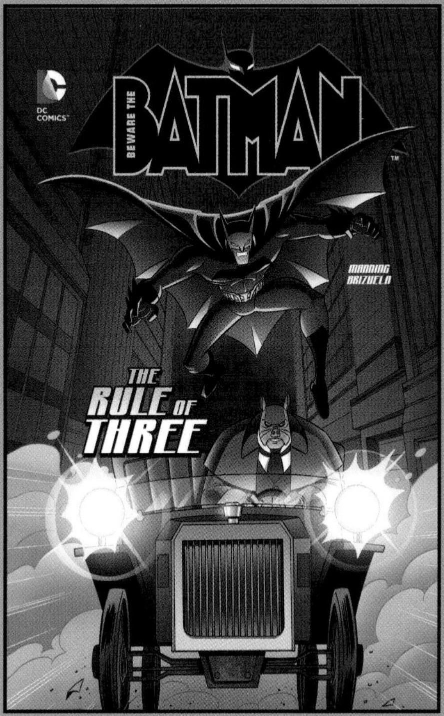
DC COMICS
BEWARE THE
BATMAN
MANNING
BRIZUELA
THE
RULE OF
THREE

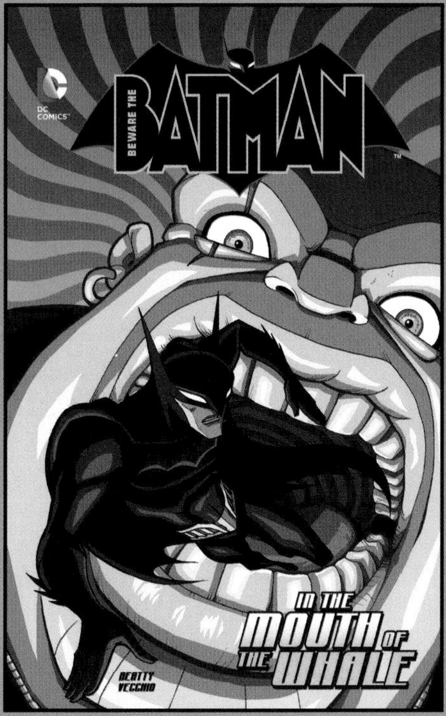
DC COMICS
BEWARE THE
BATMAN
IN THE
MOUTH OF
THE WHALE
BEATTY
VECCHIO

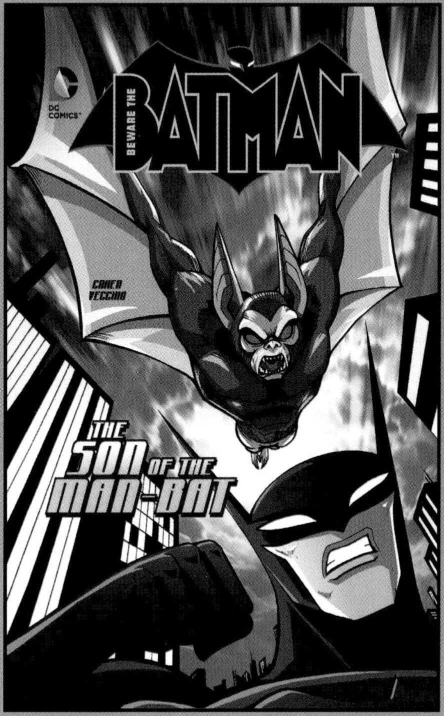
DC COMICS
BEWARE THE
BATMAN
COHEN
VECCHIO
THE
SON OF THE
MAN-BAT

BEWARE THE BATMAN™

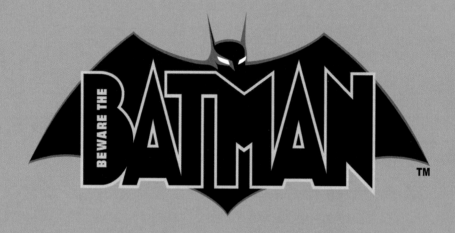